Something About a Hot Guy

C. L. Jackson

NEW YORK TIMES BESTSELLING AUTHOR

Something About a Hot Guy

More from A.L. Jackson

<u>Confessions of the Heart</u>
More of You
All of Me
Pieces of Us

<u>Fight for Me</u>
Show Me the Way
Hunt Me Down
Lead Me Home
Hold on to Hope

<u>Bleeding Stars</u>
A Stone in the Sea
Drowning to Breathe
Where Lightning Strikes
Wait
Stay
Stand

<u>The Regret Series</u>
Lost to You
Take This Regret
If Forever Comes

<u>The Closer to You Series</u>
Come to Me Quietly
Come to Me Softly
Come to Me Recklessly

<u>Stand-Alone Novels</u>
Pulled
When We Collide

one

Kenna

My fingers flew across the laptop keys. My bottom lip was tucked between my teeth in astute concentration, my attention laser-focused as I pounded out the best answer I could find to the question that had been left sometime last night.

I had to get it right.

I never wanted to mislead people or act like I had the perfect solution.

I just wanted to be honest.

Open and honest.

And sometimes that was really hard.

But that's what this was all about—cutting myself wide open and laying it out.

Giving people encouragement. Hoping they'd realize they weren't alone. See that we could all have a little fun with it along the way.

My heart raced a little harder than normal as I typed. Adrenaline always got the best of me when I got lost in the little fantasy world I'd created.

As if I were caught somewhere between a dream and reality.

That was hope, though, wasn't it? It didn't always hinge on fact. It all lived in the realm of possibility.

My phone buzzed where it sat on the floor next to me, and I grinned when I saw it was my best friend and roommate.

Vanessa: Why aren't you here? Vegas is lonely without you!

With a small smile, I shook my head. She was crazy.

Me: I promise Vegas does not miss me. Vegas and I are not friends.

Vanessa: That's because you haven't given her a chance. She's really sweet once you get to know her.

I could almost see her feigned pout from across the country. A full grin took to my mouth as I quickly replied.

Me: You also said that about the five-inch heels you tried to get me to wear out last weekend. We all know how that turned out.

It had ended with a faceplant and a bloody nose and a promise to myself to never leave the house again.

So yeah. I was a clutz. As awkward as they came, and even nerdier than that. Luckily, Vanessa still loved me for it.

Vanessa: You sell yourself short. And we miss you. A lot. It's no fun without you here.

She and our other two best friends had gone on a girls' trip. Vanessa had tried to convince me to go. She should have known me well enough to know I would have tried to sneak away to the hotel room while they were slinking off to clubs, anyway. That I felt much more comfortable in the shadows rather than traipsing around all night under the neon lights.

Me: I'm as happy as pie. Don't worry about me.

Vanessa: What flavor of pie? And just how happy is pie?

Laughter popped out. She really was crazy.

Vanessa: Seriously, I love and miss you. I wish you didn't feel the need to hide. You're way too amazing for that.

A wave of loneliness crested through my being. Sometimes I wished for that, too. That it was easier for me to step out. I was trying, but some steps were just too big, like spending a weekend out on the strip.

Bang. Bang. Bang.

At the sudden pounding at the door, my head snapped up from my phone and a high-pitched squeak escaped.

My attention flew to the open screen of my computer before it went darting around the living room as if I had gotten caught red-handed in the most salacious of acts.

I slammed down the lid in a bid to hide the evidence, set it aside, and pushed to my feet.

I tugged down my oversized sweater a little farther and fumbled across the living room, doing my best to still my rattled nerves.

For real—it was ridiculous that I reacted this way. That one single thing out of order, out of the expected, and anxiousness was making a play to ruin my day.

I was working on that. Embracing who I was and improving upon her, at the same time.

Chances were, it was someone making a delivery or trying to sell something, anyway. I didn't need to get spun up over a little knocking.

With all the confidence I had, I popped up to peek through the peephole.

Oh, and there my confidence went. Bursting like a balloon cuddling up with a barbed-wire fence.

At the fuzzy sight, my heart sputtered, my knees went weak, and a whole sea of sweat gathered on the nape of my neck.

Oh my God.

Oh no.

Pulse racing, I tried to control my breaths that had started to come short and choppy.

I was gonna have a panic attack.

I sank back down onto my heels, attention darting from side-to-side, searching for an escape, only to jump about ten feet in the air when another round of battering took to the door. Only this time it was accompanied by a rough, "Open up."

Silky and hard.

Was that even possible?

Okay, I had more important things to do than ponder the sexy tenor of his voice. Like figuring out how in the world I was going to get out of this.

"If you're trying to go covert, you're failing. I *can* hear you. Open up."

Crap.

All the craps.

Fisting my hands, I attempted to even out my breathing, play it cool (yeah right), and I bit down on my bottom lip. Shaking out of control, I reached out to turn the lock.

Warily, I cracked the door open an inch, only wide enough to peer out with one eye.

A big hand lifted and nudged the door open farther, sending me stumbling back.

Remember those weak knees? They just about fully gave up on me.

Blood drained from my head in favor of going for a stampede through my body, head rushed with a bout of dizziness and stupidity, spiraling me into that fantasy world where I liked to live before I could stop it.

It was all mixed up with the anxiety that raced and sped, hitting my limbs at full blast. It was a reaction I always had when I got nervous, tripping all over myself, nothing but a fidgeting, clumsy mess.

My mouth went completely dry, and I was pretty sure every brain cell I had blanked out.

Well, all but the ones that were taking him in as if he were a storm rising over a drought-parched desert.

Coming at full force.

"W-w-hat are you doing here?" I stuttered.

Kyle Love was standing in my doorway.

My best friend's big brother.

In the flesh.

In all the glorious, gorgeous flesh that made up that six-foot-two body. All lean, sinewy muscle and easy arrogance that made his masculine face almost appear cute.

Dark eyes swept me. Head to toe. Way slower than seemed necessary. Chills of distress and attraction crawled across my flesh, as if all those feelings I'd tried to keep contained were climbing out from the recesses.

Oh God, I was going to pass out.

"Well, if it isn't Kenna Myer. All grown up." He said my name like a tease, smooth and soft and mocking.

I hadn't seen him in two years. Not since mine and Vanessa's college graduation. He'd come to our hometown for the ceremony and party afterward.

That was where I had my last memory of him.

This guy who'd been my first crush.

There was a reason they called it that, you know? When you got crushed for the first time, you got completely obliterated. Smashed. Demolished in a way you never could have anticipated.

Since then, I'd avoided him at all costs. It'd become my superpower. Only I hadn't seen this encounter coming, and I was left without backups.

A smirk ticked up at the corner of his mouth.

"You look surprised. Weren't expecting me?"

I could feel my own lips parting in response, dropping open as I thought about what it might be like to experience those lips against mine.

I bet they tasted as good as they looked.

Heat flashed and something heavy rolled around in my belly.

Damn it. Get yourself together, Kenna. You aren't ever gonna know how that mouth tastes.

Because I was Kenna Myer and he was Kyle-Freaking-Love.

Because he was so out of my league that it caused me physical pain to look at him.

Regret and want twisted through my insides, and I shifted uneasily on my feet, fiddling with my hands, not sure what to do with them.

I needed to get him out of here and fast.

"Kyle. What are you doing here?" This time, I managed to make it come out like a demand.

That smirk ticked up higher, and he leaned against the door jamb as if he owned the place.

Oh, that's right, he did.

Vanessa and I were only leasing the apartment from him while he was out of the country.

And there he was, filling up the doorway with those wide shoulders and massive presence.

He arched a cocky brow. "What, you act like you aren't happy to see me?"

Oh, was that ever a loaded question.

I fumbled back a step, needing to get free of the force that surrounded him.

Magnetic.

The man so compelling it felt impossible to look away, every loaded second drawing me in, my entire being attracted to his essence.

A couple seconds more, and he'd have to pry me off. I bet he'd love that.

"Um . . . well . . . Vanessa isn't here," I stammered. "She's gone for the weekend. You'll have to come back on Monday."

A grin cracked his face, and his expression lifted in a challenge. "I'm afraid that's going to be a problem."

He glanced at the big bag he'd dropped on the ground at his feet, then returned the force of his gaze to me. Again, those brown eyes were taking a path over my body, gliding from my head and traipsing down.

It felt like a slow-slide of interrogation.

What in the world was he doing?

Redness clawed over every inch of my skin, and I was just then noting that I wasn't wearing a bra, one of the shoulders of my sweatshirt draped off one side, my shorts so short under it that I bet it looked like I wasn't wearing any at all.

My hair was ratted up in a messy twist high up on top of my head, a clump of toothpaste dried on the zit on my forehead.

Kill me now.

Clumsy, clueless, Kenna.

It's what he'd call me every time I'd come stumbling into their kitchen, getting all out of sorts when I'd find him sitting at their high bar, shirtless, eating cereal like a rockstar.

Did rockstars eat cereal?

If they didn't, they should.

He was the one who'd been clueless. Clueless that he was responsible for it all, evoking that reaction. Making me nervous and needy and ruffled and flustered.

Liable to trip.

Wishing when I landed, it'd be right into his big, capable hands. At least, I'd imagined a million times just how capable those hands would be.

Dropping my head, I tried to inconspicuously rub the toothpaste from my face.

No chance he would notice, right?

I was pretty sure the only thing I managed to do was smear it.

A rough chuckle rumbled around in his chest. "Oh, Kenna . . . how I've missed you."

I was pretty sure I got whiplash when he said it with the way my head snapped up, eyes going wide with his words. Then it was me who was taking in all his glory.

"Missed me?" It was a confused murmur that escaped my tongue without my permission.

"Oh, yeah." There he went teasing me again, and there went my gaze taking him in.

Tight faded tee stretched across his broad chest and his jeans fitting him oh so right. Face chiseled and his jaw wide, stubble coating every inch.

Dark hair a mess and falling over his right eye.

Trouble to the Nth degree.

He was the definition of word porn, and it was spelled h-o-t.

One of those careless smirks that had driven me out of my mind for half my life slid onto his ridiculously gorgeous face. "Aren't you going to invite me in?"

"I'm not sure that's a good idea." It was a pained whisper, and crap, I didn't even mean to speak it, the words breaking free without my permission.

Thing was, I really couldn't imagine him walking through this door, plopping himself on my couch, and putting his feet up and making himself at home.

Or maybe I just had imagined it too many times, and it felt too surreal and impossible and perfect at the exact same time.

And there went my mind, racing into that fantasy world.

A haggard breath sucked into my lungs, and another round of redness was flushing my cheeks as embarrassment streaked through my being.

It was stupid he was the only person in the world I'd wanted to be different for. I'd tried—tried to catch his eye—but the one time I'd conjured the courage on our graduation day, he'd smashed it in a one-second blow that I was pretty sure he didn't even know he'd cast.

Light laughter tumbled from his full lips, and he set his hand on the door and pushed it open a little farther.

"Considering you're sleeping in my house, I would think that would be nice of you." Only he clearly wasn't asking.

"What are you doing back already? Shouldn't you still be overseas?" It was a last-ditch effort.

He wasn't supposed to be back for two months. The man had been off taking over the world, his start-up booming, extending to the office he'd opened in Japan. Maybe I could encourage him to go back and finish his business.

That or convince him to come back on Monday when Vanessa returned. I'd heard the Spartan down the street had really great rooms. No doubt, he'd have no trouble finding someone to share the big, comfy bed.

Hell, I'd even be willing to foot the bill.

By then, I'd have plenty of time to pack my things so I could run for safety. Because I couldn't possibly stay in the same house as the boy I'd loved since third grade. The fact he would never look at me that way just hurt too bad.

"Deal was done. I had no reason to stay, and I was missing home. Found myself on the next flight. And here I am."

He grinned a wicked grin before glancing around the apartment.

Sunlight poured in through the big windows, reflecting on the soft pink and white accents Vanessa and I had decorated the living room and kitchen in, everything cozy and bright.

He visibly cringed. "Looks like you and my sister did a number on the place."

A frown pulled to my face. "I . . . well . . . we didn't think you'd mind. We did sign a lease for two years."

He couldn't have possibly thought we would leave all his stuff out? The last thing I'd wanted was a constant reminder of him. A tease of what I couldn't have and wanted more than I ever should.

Reaching down, he plucked his bag from the ground.

"Don't mind. All the pink might have caught me off guard, but a real man can deal. And you're right. You do have the lease for two years. Don't worry, Kenna, I always keep my promises."

Why was he looking at me that way?

Intense and deep. Energy flashing through the air. Making it hard to breathe. Like maybe he wanted to reach out and touch me. Feel me the way I'd always wanted to feel him.

God, I loved to torture myself with the impossible, didn't I?

Letting my imagination get the best of me. Teasing me with what could never be. I'd already learned that the hard way.

He shouldered by, stealing my breath, the brush of our skin sending a cascade of shivers tumbling down my spine as he pushed his way into the apartment.

A waterfall pooling in the middle of me. Pounding and overflowing.

"You won't even notice I'm here."

Um, he really was the clueless one, wasn't he?

From over his shoulder, he sent me a smile that nearly dropped me to my knees, all one-sided dimple and plush lips and mischievous eyes.

"I'll sleep on the couch. And I won't make either of you pay rent for the rest of your lease, how's that sound?"

How's that sound?

It sounded like my worst nightmare.

"I'll do you a favor, and I won't even walk around in my underwear. I mean, unless you want me to."

He winked, hitting me with all that reckless easiness that punched me in the gut. A fist right through my belly and gripping my stomach in a want and desire so intense that it physically hurt.

I swayed under the force of it, and my hand darted out to the back of the couch to keep myself from faceplanting on the hardwood floor.

"You . . . you can't possibly stay here?" Panic started to set in when I realized he was serious, that this man was really going to be invading my space, my heart quickening to a boom, a deep, dark thunder rolling through my being.

"I mean, we have a whole schedule and our lives and you're . . . you're . . ."

I waved my hands in the air as if maybe that would be enough resistance to scare him away. Enough reason for him to leave.

I had to find some way to stop this from happening.

He was a danger to my sanity.

To my heart.

To my safe little world.

All it took was him stepping through the door and my entire world had become a bomb threat. I could already feel the ground trembling, sex and power and influence coming off of him in waves, so distinct I was sure you could bottle it and sell it for a billion bucks.

He'd always had that effect on me.

My senses perking whenever he came within a mile vicinity, every part of me getting needy like a lap dog that wanted to be petted.

I'd hoped once I'd moved out of our small town and into the city that it would have faded. That I would have outgrown this childish fascination.

How unfair was it that it'd only increased tenfold since he'd been away? Grown and expanded and become this palpable entity that I could feel glowing in my center. Begging for something that I could never have.

I had to get him out of there, and I had to do it fast.

He angled his head. "And I'm . . .?" he prodded when I trailed off into a stupor of silence.

"You're you." My arms flailed outward, as if I were waving the evidence of *him* in his face. "You're messy and arrogant and . . . and a boy."

"A boy, huh?" Amusement rode out on his rough words, the man so pretty and cocky and infuriating.

"Yes, yes, a boy, and boys are totally not welcome."

Oh my God.

I was twelve.

He crossed his arms over his chest, a smile twitching all over his magnificent face. "Are you finished?"

"Not even close. I mean, when we signed that lease, there was no mention that you might be back. I know it's your apartment, and all, but what . . . what if we have *company*?"

I said the last as if it were sordid. And I wondered if he had the first clue that was the farthest from the truth when it came to me. Not that he'd care. But I was pretty sure Vanessa might care if he was invading her privacy.

That's right.

I was doing this for her. For my friend who had always been there for me. At least that was what I was telling myself.

He plopped on the couch and grabbed the remote.

My mouth dropped open. "Kyle. Are you even listening to me?" I pled, feeling invisible, trying to be brave and stand up for myself.

"I'm not sure how I couldn't be, considering you won't stop talking. It's been a long flight. I could use a little quiet."

The audacity. He really was rude. How had I forgotten?

Huffing, I stamped my foot and started for him so I could grab the remote before he completely tuned me out.

I should have known better than to even move in his vicinity.

Should have known my clumsiness would get the best of me.

Because my little toe caught on the leg of the end table at the side of the couch, and oh my goodness, the pain. Splintering pain that shot up my toe and foot.

A shout of agony burst free of my mouth.

"Oh . . . shoot. Oh my goodness. Oh my . . . fuuuuudge."

I was gasping for breath as I hauled my foot up, holding it in my hands to try to ease the sharp, breathtaking pain as I hopped around erratically on one foot, flying from one side and then to the other.

Kyle shot to standing, and before I could make sense of it, those big hands were on the outside of my arms. Holding me up.

Warmth spread across my flesh.

Molten chocolate.

At least, that's what I'd always envisioned his touch would feel like. Only, it was so much better than that, fire that flamed up my skin and seeped in deep. This intense energy transferred in the connection. I wanted to melt into it. Get lost in the sensation.

Too bad I was the only one who felt the spark.

I whimpered with the pain that had started to throb, unable to stop tears from pricking at my eyes.

Leave it to me to make a complete fool of myself.

Without an ounce of effort, he lifted me by the arms and shifted me around, and he carefully sat me down on the couch.

"I think I'm dying," I cried, sure there wasn't a worse pain in all the world than stubbing your little toe.

Forget childbirth.

Or maybe I was just dying of embarrassment.

"Are you all right?" There was no missing the bit of laughter he was holding back as he knelt down in front of me.

Groaning, I threw my arm over my eyes. "No. I think I broke it. And don't laugh at me."

"You didn't break it." He tsked a little, and it was low and soft and made all kinds of funny things happen in my belly that I definitely shouldn't be feeling right then. Especially with the way he was right there, in my space, the man prying my foot from my hold and cradling it in his hands.

Heat flamed, glowing from within, filling me with need, my

thighs shaking with something else entirely than the anxiety that loved to hold me prisoner.

Studying my foot, he winced. "Shit . . . you did a number on this. It's already swollen."

My eyes flew open. "Are you serious? Oh, no . . . it's broken, isn't it? Why does this always happen to me?"

"Let me get some ice. Sit tight."

"Like I'm going anywhere."

He climbed to standing, though he didn't move away. He just leaned over me, his presence thick and massive and overwhelming, so much so that my chest heaved with a needy pant. His mouth came up close to my ear. "And neither am I."

Shivers raced, stealing the blood from my head, replacing it with a swell of lightheadedness that wooshed through my senses.

Leaving me weak.

I tried to gather myself when he moved for the kitchen, all that cool easiness radiating from every step he took. Desperately, I tried not to stare over the back of the couch as he sauntered to the refrigerator, but there was nothing I could do but watch as he moved.

Confidence oozing from that body.

So easy.

Easy in a way I'd never known.

He filled a zippy bag with ice while I sat there shaking with apprehension, hating that I was this way. For just one day, I wanted to be normal. Confident and strong and brave.

Sexy.

Wield the kind of power this man wielded over me.

Just as fast as he'd gone, he was back with a dishtowel wrapped around the bag. He returned to kneeling in front of me, careful as he placed the bag on my aching toe.

I flinched at the cold, then gave in as he spread a big hand around my ankle and gently pressed the cold pack to my toe.

"There we go."

Unable to bear his proximity, I reached for it.

Kyle nudged my hand away. "I've got it."

"I can take care of myself," I whispered, realizing I was

begging. That I needed him to understand I couldn't be this close to him and not feel as if I were coming apart. Missing something that I'd wanted for far too long.

Loving someone from afar was the cruelest sort of penalty. Watching them go on without you as if they'd never noticed you were there in the first place.

Rough laughter scraped up his throat. "Clueless Kenna."

A hurt breath left me, and the tears I'd been trying not to cry welled in my eyes. I couldn't believe he would still call me that. After all this time. What was more disturbing was that it still affected me this way.

He resituated my leg, propping it up on the couch and tucking a pillow under my ankle. My lungs squeezed in pain, and I was barely able to inhale, wondering how he could put me down and then take care of me so tenderly in the same breath.

That gaze swept up, dark eyes penetrating, and those shallow breaths raking from my lungs completely stalled out.

His mouth twisted up in a way that took my insides with it, everything getting tangled and tight, and he reached up and brushed back a piece of hair that had fallen in my face, his expression different than I'd ever seen it before.

His tongue swept across his plump bottom lip, the words a low, seductive rasp. "Clueless, Clueless Kenna."

two

Kyle

Clueless Kenna.

Clueless, awkward, sexy-as-fuck Kenna.

She was killing me.

Breaths coming from her lush mouth in these rough, choppy pants, the girl pinned under me on the couch, those brown eyes wide and unsure.

No doubt, I was making things up, but I could have sworn I saw them flaming with desire, too.

"Please, don't call me that," she whispered, her chest shaking.

Did she actually think I was putting her down?

A smile pulled to my mouth, and fuck yeah, I'd teased her growing up. That's what boys did when they crushed on a girl so hard they went stupid.

"And what would you like me to call you?"

Baby sounded about right.

"My name works just fine. I do at least understand that."

Apparently, she didn't have the first clue how damn appealing that she was. Had anyone ever told her?

I'd nearly come undone when she'd opened the door, standing there in what I was pretty sure was a man's sweatshirt that swallowed her whole.

Instantly, I was hard. Mind running with the idea that she didn't have a stitch on underneath.

Completely bare.

Tits puckered and needy. As needy as the sweet spot between her thighs. Didn't even care that she had toothpaste dried on her forehead.

But half the time, it felt like she despised me. Like she wanted to split the second we got in the same room.

Which had always gotten to me since she was the kindest person I'd ever met. I'd spent years watching her give and give and give. Girl would ignore the insults and abuse and snubs that assholes would cast her way, turning right around and pouring out her goodness into the world when it didn't deserve to receive the genuine inner beauty of this girl.

Was I that bad of a guy that I didn't deserve any of that?

The fact my sister would cut my balls off if I even thought about touching her best friend only came in as a close second.

Only I thought about it.

A lot.

"How about . . . Cupcake Kenna?" That sounded nice, right? Not too forward? Because I was thinking she might not take too kindly to something along the lines of *I want to get lost in your sweet cunt Kenna.*

Too far?

Yeah.

She rolled her eyes like she thought I was mocking her.

If she only knew.

And now I was really, really hungry for a cupcake.

Fuck my life.

My tongue darted out to wet my lips, and I hovered, wavered, relished in the feel of her heart beating wild in the bare space between us.

Shit. I wanted to kiss her. Climb onto this couch and crawl all over her. Take her hard and then take her slow.

Like she saw the intention written on me, panic surged through her expression, and she started to fidget and get all flustered in that adorable way that set her apart from everyone.

She pressed her hand against my chest, then she jerked her hand away, like she'd thought better of that, too. "I'm fine now, Kyle. Honest. I've got it. You don't have to worry about me."

There she went, pushing me away, though when she did it, I swore I heard an undercurrent of sadness lacing the words.

I wanted to grab her hand and lock it to my chest so she could feel the crazy thing going down inside. So she could feel the way she affected me. Desperate to know if there was any chance she might feel the least bit the same.

Had told myself not to think about her on my way back to the States. Told myself it was never going to happen. To fucking forget it.

But that didn't come close to stopping the fantasies from assaulting me. The feelings that annihilated me the second I saw her standing at the door.

"What if I've always worried about you?"

A frown pulled across her brow. "You've always been full of yourself, Kyle Love, but I never took you for a liar."

It was my turn to frown. "You really think I don't care about you? You've been Vanessa's best friend since you were a little girl. You're basically family."

She shifted her gaze away when I claimed it, like maybe she didn't know how to accept that truth.

My sister was crazy protective over her. I got why. Those nasty bitches in high school couldn't exactly be considered *nice*. I'd gone to bat for her more than a couple of times, though I doubted it made any difference. Mean girls were always mean girls. Fucking sucked, but that was the life of high school, wasn't it?

But we weren't in high school anymore. Hadn't been for a long time. And Kenna? Even amid all that bullshit? She'd still been generous to everyone. Kind and considerate and thoughtful. Going out of her way to make someone smile.

Yeah.

She was drop-dead gorgeous. The kind of girl that would make me trip all over myself. But it was her humility that had always made her shine. It was the way she'd stop to take care of a stranger without thought. The way she'd go out of her way to do the right thing, without asking for anything in return.

She was the real deal.

A scowl pulled to her adorable face, turned-up nose and full cheeks, a pink bow for lips.

She laughed a disbelieving sound. "You don't have to pity me, Kyle. I get it. And I'm fine. Just . . . go do your thing, and I'll do mine. I'll be sure to get out of your way as soon as I can."

This time, I did grab her hand, holding it tight. Heat licked and flamed. I was a second from losing it, confessing every fucking thing that I kept bottled up tight. "I'm not here to kick you out of your own damn apartment. You're staying."

She pried her hand free, a look I couldn't make out crossing her face. "One of us is leaving."

I guessed she really did hate me. Had no idea what I'd done, but I'd seen the way she'd looked at me for all those years.

Like just being in my presence made her want to puke.

Let me tell you, it made a teenaged boy feel super awesome. Did wonders for his self-confidence.

While other girls were throwing themselves at me, the one I wanted wouldn't even look me in the eye. On some level, I got that she was shy, but the man in me hadn't gotten it at all.

Frustration bled into my bones, and I edged up closer, getting right in her face. "Sorry, cupcake, but that's not gonna happen. This is your home, and you're not going anywhere. And I'm not going anywhere, either. Get used to it."

A smirk ticked up on the corner of my mouth, and I tried to lighten the mood that was feeling far too heavy. "Besides, what would I do with all this pink shit?"

Hesitation brimmed around her before a small smile was pulling at the corner of her mouth. "I guess I would have to take it with me. Although I'm pretty sure your sister would fight me over it. You know how much she hates people messing with her things."

For the first time, there was a softness to her words, and it made me feel like a king that maybe my attempt had worked.

"I bet she would. Every time I even touched her toys as a kid, she lost her mind." Affection filled my voice. "You'd have thought

I'd started a world war when I hid her Barbie dolls."

A hint of amusement touched her cheeks, her shyness so damn sweet. "I'm pretty sure that might have had something to do with the fact that when we found them, they all were wearing the wrong heads. Poor Ken had boobs."

"Never said I wasn't creative."

"Creative? I'd call that psychotic. Dismembering poor, innocent dolls. Isn't that a sign of a horrible disorder?"

God, she was cute when she was playful. When she let go a little bit.

I could feel the wistful grin tugging at my mouth as I stared down at her. Getting lost in those brown eyes, in the way they flitted over my face, jumping from my eyes to my mouth and away, like she didn't know where to look.

Shit, I wanted to lean in closer. Drink her in.

Dip in. Dive in.

I edged closer. Closer and closer.

Fuck.

If I erased any more space between us, I'd be crawling on top of her, pushing her over a line she clearly didn't want me crossing.

I stood before I did something stupid.

"So . . . what do you want to do today?"

Smooth, Kyle. Smooth. You'd think I was back to being fifteen rather than a twenty-seven-year-old man. But when it came to Kenna? The rules went out the window. The girl different than any other woman I'd dealt with before.

Her attention darted to the computer sitting on the coffee table. Almost like she was terrified of it. She peeked up at me. "I have work to do."

Right.

Vanessa had told me Kenna taught on-line school because she had trouble standing in front of a group of people. Fucking sucked. I mean, I respected her choice. Got it on some level. But it had to be brutal, completely exhausting, letting your fears rule your life.

I glanced around, wanting to say things I probably shouldn't say. To tell her she was amazing and wonderful, tell her about all the things I'd observed over the years that made her the best person I'd ever met, and that it was time she shed that shell, embraced who she was.

But did I really have the right to give that kind of advice when I'd never had to walk in her shoes?

I needed to get away from this girl before I kept pushing it. Hell, I'd been back for all of five minutes, and I'd already pushed her harder than I ever had. Climbed right over the boundaries I'd set up when it came to Kenna Myer.

Maybe I was just tired of ignoring the way I felt about her. No matter how many girlfriends I'd had, how many one-nights and flings, this feeling didn't seem to know how to go away.

"All right, then . . . I'm going to grab a shower and let you get to work."

Redness streaked up her cheeks, and I got the sense that she was actually imagining me naked.

Fuck.

Not helping things.

"I'll try to stay out of your way."

She looked at me like she thought I was telling her a lie. Two of us completely aware of the other. Every step and every breath.

And I was wondering again if maybe she felt me, too.

I grabbed my bag from the floor and headed for the shower, turned on the heat as high as it would go, and climbed into the steam surrounded by the scent of citrus and more of the pink she'd decorated the place in.

And I jerked it harder than I ever had.

So, the jerking off hadn't helped my situation at all.

I'd tried to keep myself occupied the entire day, let her work in peace as she'd graded freshman language arts essays. She'd sat on the couch with the sunlight pouring over her, her laptop balanced on her crisscrossed legs, the girl looking like she was posing for some some kind of perfect Instagram shot.

Hashtag hot nerd.

I'd pretended to be busy on my own laptop at the small kitchen table, answering emails and scheduling appointments for next week, but my attention kept drifting to her. Getting locked on the soft profile of her face. At the way the lush dark locks tumbled down her neck. At the way she moved her lips as she read the essays, so into it, I could almost feel her vibrating.

Once the sun had dimmed and begun to set, I'd ordered a pizza for us to share after she'd explained she still had a couple hours left of work.

Now, I brushed my teeth and pulled on some sleep pants, figuring I'd make good on my promise about not walking around in my underwear, all the while wondering what she might do if I threw all rationale out the window and went for it.

Blowing out a strained sigh toward the mirror, I tried to shake off the disorder I was feeling. I'd barely been here a day, and this was already proving impossible.

I headed out into the hall. Her bedroom door was resting open on the jamb, a light burning around the rim. She was probably in there, changing, getting ready to climb under the covers.

I could only picture her doing it. Bare legs and full breasts and messy hair.

Shit.

I wasn't really up-to-date with proper roommate etiquette, but I was pretty sure picturing them naked was a no-go.

Slipping by her door, I turned the corner into the main room, heading for the kitchen to grab one of the beers I'd seen in there earlier. Most of the lights had been cut, the space only illuminated by the dim lights mounted under the cabinets.

My heart jumped into my throat when I noticed the silhouette of a body standing at the sink facing away.

A lush, curved, gorgeous body.

I kept my footsteps quiet as I started around the high bar that sectioned off the kitchen from the living room. She was gulping down a glass of water, totally oblivious to the fact that I was there.

Until she wasn't.

Until her spine stiffened and awareness flooded from her in

surging waves, a vibration coming off her that made me question if I really was the only one who felt this crazy attraction.

If I was the only one who was crazy with lust.

Crazy with need.

She was still wearing the sweatshirt that fell off one shoulder, the delicate skin of her neck bare.

I had the overwhelming urge to press my nose to the slope of it. Inhale and lick and suck.

Instead, I kept myself in check and stopped an inch away.

Okay, in check was stretching it because I leaned. So close I could almost taste her flesh, the aura of this girl making me feel like I was standing in the sun.

I inhaled, filling my lungs with her scent.

Clean, crisp lime wrapped in vanilla.

Like she'd rolled around in a bed of those little white blossoms.

Shit, I wanted to do a little *rolling around*, too.

"Kenna." Her name was a rough plea from my mouth.

Do you feel this?

Shivers tremored through her body, rising across her flesh, and she slowly turned around. Immediately, she backed into the counter, not shocked to find me there but somehow terrified at the same time.

She swiped the back of her hand over the droplets of water that clung to her lips.

An impossibly sexy move that she had no idea she'd perfected.

"Hey, K-k-kyle . . . I . . . I was just going to bed," she said, flustered and sweet and shy. I wanted to dip my fingers into the well of it, stir it up, watch her bloom.

She started to slide out around me. I stepped in her way. Her eyes widened with surprise. A timid animal that was trapped.

I cleared my throat, not sure what to say, but knowing I needed to give her something.

I'd waltzed in like an arrogant dick. Making demands. But I knew her well enough to know she would have sent me packing if I'd given her another option.

"I just wanted to tell you how much I appreciate you being cool with me being here."

Incredulity filled her eyes. "You didn't leave me much of a choice, did you?"

I angled my head her direction. "You really want me to leave? If you really, really want me to go, say it, and I will. Don't get me wrong, I want to stay."

Fuck, I wanted to stay.

"But if you really don't want to be around me that bad? I'll leave right now."

Distress swirled around her being, the girl squirming, casting her gaze away before she finally looked back up at me. "No. I really don't. It's just sometimes hard for me to accept strangers being in my space."

I inched closer, eradicating all but a breadth between us, the air growing dense and thick. A frenzy of energy swirled around her, nerves and anxiousness, and I swore, need.

I could taste it.

Feel it.

Wanted to drown in it.

I dipped in closer. "Kenna. You think I'm a stranger?"

I said it like a question. Hoping to God she'd take the step, make the move, or at least give me some kind of indication she might want me the way I wanted her.

Tell me that she recognized *me*.

Panic parted her mouth, and she swallowed hard. Then she fumbled to duck out from under me, spinning around with her hands pushed out like a shield between us. "I, um, so . . . I need to go to bed. Goodnight."

She spun back around so fast that she tripped over her feet, stumbling forward, catching herself just before she fell. Her hand went up to tug at a piece of hair that had gotten loose from the pile on top of her head, embarrassment radiating from her as she beelined for her room.

The door clicked shut with a finality that had me pressing my hands to my face, wanting to punch myself in my own dick.

That did not go well.

God damn it.

Frustrated, I went for the fridge. Jerking open the door, I

grabbed a bottle and popped off the cap. I tossed it into the trash and started to head out, only to pause when I noticed she'd left her laptop sitting on the counter.

Open an inch.

Like she'd still been working on it and carried it in while she got a drink of water.

I glanced over my shoulder, wondering if I should take it to her.

Hell, knowing I should.

I angled back so I could see down the short hall, and the light had gone off in her room.

Guessed that was all the go I needed to start nudging the screen up, just a fraction, wanting to feel closer to her, understand her better, maybe read one of the essays that had entranced her all day so I could see exactly what it was that made her tick. What put those twitchy, adorable smiles on her face and made her teeth clamp down on her bottom lip.

Okay, fine, I was being a nosy fucker.

My brow pinched when I caught a glimpse of what was on the screen.

Not an essay.

Pulse thudding, I glanced over my shoulder again, wondering what the fuck I was doing when I lifted the lid the rest of the way.

The words glowing on the screen came into full view.

I scanned over them.

It was a blog, and a recent post was up, an answer to a question that had been posted left halfway completed, the curser still blinking like a beacon in the night, something about dealing with social fear and how it can be debilitating.

What the fuck?

Unease curled through my being, and I knew I should slam it closed, but there was nothing I could do but note the blog website address as I lowered the screen to where it'd been left.

I should let it go. I knew I should. But there was an itching inside of me that couldn't be contained, and I opened my phone and pulled up the website as I moved back to the couch. I sank down onto the blanket I'd dragged out from the hall closet and ticked into another blog post.

I read it.

Then I read another.

And another.

Until hours had passed and my mind spun and my spirit thrashed.

I got lost as I read about a girl who was beautiful in every way.

Inside and out.

Just like I'd always known she'd been. What had really attracted me to her in the first place. That shy beauty ushering me up to a cliff and her kindness pushing me over the edge.

A girl who confessed to being fearful and anxious and prone to panic attacks in large groups.

Giving and loving and hopeful in spite of it all.

A girl who had grown into a woman who had managed to get her teaching degree despite her worry and doubt.

Hand shaking, I clicked into another post, titled Something About a Hot Guy. I wanted to cringe, knowing I was really invading her privacy as she opened up about her trouble meeting men. How she confessed to being a virgin because she didn't have the first clue how to get close to a man, let alone, let one touch her.

Then I tripped over the next words, heart pressing against my ribs so hard I was pretty sure I heard a crack.

Words that said she was in love with her best friend's big brother, and being unable to admit it was killing her inside.

Fuck me.

three

Kenna

Would it be weird if I stayed in bed all day? I mean, it was Saturday. That would be cool, right? Except I'd been staring at the ceiling for the last . . . sixty-seven minutes . . . three minutes more than the last time I looked at the clock.

Two more minutes of this, and I would lose my mind.

I'd left my computer in the kitchen last night, too much of a chicken to go back out to grab it when I realized I'd left it sitting next to the sink.

Crap.

I flung off my covers with the dramatic flair of one of my freshmen high-school students, and I jumped from the bed, only to slow, slinking to the bathroom across the hall all ninja-like. As if I were the intruder rather than the other way around.

It didn't really matter.

I could feel him the second I opened the door, a surge of energy that crashed through the morning air, filled with intensity and zest and life.

Kyle Love was the kind of guy who could reach out and take the world in the palm of his hand. Stretch it out and all the amazing things would intrinsically be drawn to him.

Dull, frumpy, awkward things, too.

I raced through my morning routine because I definitely didn't want him to think I was in there doing *you know what*, cringing at the thought, self-conscious and unsure as I edged back out toward the kitchen.

I breathed a sigh of relief when I saw that he was out on the balcony, a cup of coffee in hand as he leaned on the railing, his back bare and delicious and muscular as he stared out over the bustling city below.

Oh God.

He was magnificent.

A god who'd descended on the common folk.

Want tremored through me like an earthquake. Shaking through my being. Strong enough that it threatened to fracture the thin threads that held my safe, little world together.

I allowed myself creeper status for exactly five seconds, swallowing down the sight of him and filing it away in all the reasons Kyle Love was five-thousand miles out of my league.

My mind was only taunting me last night, torturing me with the idea that he might see me differently. That he might want me the way I wanted him.

Prying myself from the morning view, I headed into the kitchen, in dire need of one of those cups of coffee he was nursing. I fumbled for a cup in the cupboard, trying to keep my hand from shaking all over the place when a rash of goosebumps skidded across my flesh when a shadow fell over me from behind.

The same way as it had done last night. Only this time . . . this time it felt entirely different. This time, something about it felt unstoppable. Overwhelming and crushing and irresistible.

My shoulders curled in as if I were trying to find a place to hide, but there was no place I could go. Nothing I could do to escape the magnitude of him inching up behind me, his steps slow and somehow purposed.

I sucked in a staggered breath, then all the air whooshed from my lungs when he set a hand on my neck and pressed his cheek to the opposite side, right up close to my temple.

Sensation rushed.

Overwhelming.

Delicious and decadent and dizzying.

I had to be dreaming.

That was it. I was still in bed, finally succumbing to the tossing and turning that had kept me up all night, lost to the idea of the man who had to be asleep on the couch and not currently touching me.

Right?

Only this felt real. So freaking real.

"Kenna," Kyle murmured, low and rough, and even in my inexperience, I was pretty sure it was loaded with seduction.

A rash of chills shuddered through my entire being.

"Do you have any idea how beautiful you are?" His lips whispered across my skin, and I was sucking for air, trying not to pass out.

I wanted to reject it and accept it. Push away and fall into his arms at the same time. This felt . . . dangerous. Dangerous and perfect and more than anything I'd ever felt.

I swayed under the magnitude of it, and he edged even closer, keeping me pinned with my belly against the counter to keep me from falling.

His hard, hard body molded to my back.

Nothing had ever felt so good.

A big hand came to my shoulder, skimming down my arm. Chills crashed like waves climbing the beach, rising higher.

A desperate, shaky feeling seeped all the way into my blood stream.

Pulse wild, a thunder that was riding completely out of control.

Kyle's tone deepened, the man inundating every sense. "I bet you don't have the first clue, do you? How gorgeous you are? How people turn their heads every time you walk down the sidewalk because there is just something special about you? Something beautiful and bright and inspiring?"

"I . . ." I couldn't form a response, couldn't process what he was saying.

Was he really saying he thought I was beautiful? Did he really mean it? Or was this the cruelest prank that had ever been played on me? God knew, I'd endured some brutal ones.

He feathered those lips down the column of my neck, and my heart took flight. Shooting into orbit. I was pretty sure I was floating with it. No gravity left to keep me grounded.

"I bet you look in the mirror, and you don't see what the rest of the world sees. What I see."

He nuzzled his nose along my jaw. "*What I've always seen.*"

The last was raw and grating. Penetrating all the way to the soul.

Tremors took hold, nerves and anxiety and need. It was the last that was blooming bright, sprinting out in front of the others, my belly tightening and my heart battering against my ribs.

I wanted him.

I wanted this.

And for the first time in my life, I didn't feel like I was freaking out by the brush of a hand. This felt . . . safe. Safe and right and terrifying.

I wanted to tap into the feeling, make it a part of me, keep it forever.

I sagged against his chest, giving him permission to touch me however he wanted, praying that would be everywhere, and he spread his hands down my sides and tucked me closer. "Did you know that, cupcake? Did you know I spent my whole life wanting you? Wondering what your little hands would feel like on my body. What your mouth would feel like on mine. The way you'd *taste*."

The last evoked an embarrassing moan I stood no chance of holding back, a fire lit in the middle of me, flames licking up and scorching all those places a man had never been.

"Did you feel it, too?" Kyle pressed, his hands cinching down tighter on my hips.

His hardness pressed to my lower back, and a gasp was escaping, shock and desire and confusion.

Was this really happening?

My head nodded where it rested on the thunder of his heart, my admission locked in my throat, but my body shouting it from the rooftops.

I felt it. Oh God, I felt it in a way I'd never felt anything else.

"Say it," he demanded, and he slowly turned me around, taking my face in the well of those big, big hands. Intense brown eyes stared down at me.

Trapping me.

Taking me.

Owning me.

"I want to hear you say it, Kenna. I don't want there to be any mistake. Not about the way you feel, and not about the way I feel."

Anxiety fluttered and flapped, a buzz in my brain that wanted to take hold the way it always did, but this mattered too much. Was too important. The thing I'd wanted most. No chance was I letting my insecurities get in the way.

"I . . . I've always wanted you, Kyle." The words were a choppy wheeze, a confession that rose from my spirit and tumbled from my tongue. My tongue darted out to wet my dry lips, and I did my best to keep it together.

To be honest.

To tear away the layers that kept everything veiled and offer them to him.

"The first time I saw you was the first time I felt butterflies, and those butterflies have never, ever gone away."

It'd been as if he'd inspired them to awaken, spread their wings, and leave their cocoons. I'd also been a little horrified of the reaction, thinking that *funny* feeling was something bad, and I should hide it.

Right then, I didn't feel like hiding.

A tender smile that somehow still oozed of sex pulled across his lush mouth, his lips so full, his own tongue sweeping out as if his mouth were watering. "That makes me very, very happy to hear, cupcake."

There he went, calling me names again, although this name made me feel hot inside, something gooey and needy and wild twisting through my body and tightening into a ball of need.

I bit down on my bottom lip to stop the blush, staring up at those brown eyes that were hypnotizing me.

As if they had the power to turn me into someone different.

Someone confident and pretty and brave.

Or maybe it was even powerful enough to peel back the layers to expose what was waiting to be discovered underneath.

"How so?" Was that almost a tease coming from my mouth?

A grin spread across his gorgeous face, and he brushed his thumb across my lips. "Because now . . . now I'm going to kiss you like I've been wanting to do for years. And then I'm going to undress you so I can adore this gorgeous body. From there? It's up to you."

My heart squeezed, a prisoner to his hand, all the love I'd felt for this man rising to the surface. Getting ready to make a break. But would he accept it? The significance of what I felt? For me, this went so much farther beyond the physical.

But oh my God, did I want that, too.

Cockiness deepened that grin, one eye arching as he looped a strong arm around my waist. "As long as you're cool with that?"

My throat felt achy and raw, wobbling with a need I hadn't ever felt before. "I think I'm very, very cool with that." Only, I was pretty sure I was the least bit *cool* I'd ever been, the words quaking as they trembled out.

Nerves rattled, need racing, my limbs heavy and achy.

He threaded his fingers through my hair, and my eyes dropped closed, and I luxuriated in the feel of a man touching me in a way that I'd never been touched.

Tenderly and with reverence.

And there was a part of me that wanted to shout out for him to wait. To explain that I'd never even been kissed, but his gaze struck me mute, stole the words from my mouth just as he was pressing his mouth to mine.

Gently.

Sweetly.

As if he already got it.

Understood me in a way no other person did.

A tiny squeak of shock climbed my throat at the contact, sparks and delirium and joy. My hands shook, and I had no idea what to do with them, but I figured placing them against his rock-hard chest was a good start.

His skin was warm and smooth and all kinds of solid underneath. I could die a happy girl right then, getting to experience this.

The feel of this man beneath my palms. The feel of his heart thundering, the flexing and bowing of his muscles at my touch. All mixed up with the intoxicating feel of his lips moving over mine.

A hand went to the back of my head, and he angled to the side, taking that mind-altering kiss deeper.

Invading.

Conquering all my fears.

A gasp raked down my throat, and I was opening my mouth.

A gush of desire flooded my body when he swept his tongue against mine.

Soft and languid. Yet somehow those gentle strokes were a command.

His mouth was the most delicious place I'd ever been. I wanted to stay there forever, and it was as if he knew because he was taking that kiss to a new level. His lips pressing and pulling and sucking, overwhelming in their pursuit of me, his tongue plundering and invading.

Warmth flooded through my body, that waterfall hit with a flashflood, everything pouring over. Pounding, pounding, pounding.

An empty, achiness blossomed in my belly, begging for him to take it away. To fill it up. To keep it forever.

Shock rasped from my lungs when he suddenly hoisted me from my feet and propped me on the counter, and somehow my legs were parting, making him room.

Instinct kicking in, all too eager to welcome him into the cove between my thighs. Another mortifying moan left me when he pressed the long, hard length of him to my center, his sleep pants thin and my shorts thinner, and oh my God, this feeling built inside of me.

Built and built and built as he rubbed against me.

Something so big and intense that I thought I was going to burst and die.

"Kyle . . . oh . . . what." My fingers sank into his shoulders, holding on for dear life because I wanted to live for this.

Forever and ever.

I beat back the insecurities that this was a one-time thing. The worry that maybe he thought hooking up with me might be easy. Convenient since we were staying in the same house.

Even if it was, I knew I'd willingly give up anything to get to experience this with him.

All my firsts.

My trust given to him.

Praying even if he left me it wouldn't break me in the end.

"I've got you, sweet girl. Don't worry." He was kissing me madly, his tongue devouring, the man taking the kiss down my chin and across my jaw, riding down my trembling throat.

He fed on it, his breaths coming shorter and shorter, as if maybe he wanted this as badly as me. "I've got you. I'm going to take care of you. I get it. I get it now."

I could feel the frown pulling to my brow, but I tried to ignore it, the ripple of unease that billowed through my senses.

"You're so brave. So brave."

The confusion sharpened, and I tried to get lost in the feel of his hands that were slipping under my sweatshirt, firm and fierce and possessive. My hands curled in his hair as he kissed across my exposed collarbone, his chin nudging the fabric farther and farther down until he was licking across my breast that ached, wanting more of him.

But his words screamed in my mind.

"Brave? Why would say that?"

Why did he go from teasing me last night to pushing it this morning? My thoughts raced, knocking me out of the passion, something yucky riding in to take its place.

"Who you are makes you brave. The fact you're scared and anxious and go through all that bullshit you don't deserve, and still you survive. That you continue to try to make the world a better place even after it's been so cruel to you."

His words were sweet, but they gave me pause, made me question. Made fear and hurt and rejection come barreling in.

Every insecurity I ever had flared. The feeling that no one would really ever see me for me.

Awareness sank to the pit of my stomach.

Dousing the fire.

My attention locked on my computer that still sat in the same place as it had last night. But I was certain it sat opened a fraction wider.

Horror and embarrassment and anger jumped into my veins, a disorder of hurt that sped and thrashed and crushed.

It raced to fill every cell with a sort of anguish I'd never experienced before. I was gasping, my sight fading, my heart feeling like it might rupture from the blow.

Kyle seemed to sense it. He edged back in a flash, that gorgeous face twisted in confusion and worry and lust, the man watching me with concern.

The air between us throbbed, thick and dense and deep.

Binding us together and somehow pushing us apart.

"Tell me why you're saying that," I pleaded, already knowing what he would say.

"I . . . I—" He hesitated, averting his gaze, and I just knew.

I just knew.

Humiliation stampeded through my spirit.

Devastating. Crushing. Cutting me in two.

"Tell me you didn't."

He roughed a hand through his hair, and finally he returned that intense gaze to me. "I . . . I'm sorry. I just caught a glimpse . . ."

A glimpse.

It sounded to me as if he knew a whole lot more.

As if he'd pried and overstepped.

Disrespected my privacy.

Betrayed the trust I'd been so willing to give.

The only thing I'd ever wanted was for him to want me for me.

Tears broke free, and I started to squirm, struggling to get out of his hold, needing get away from him before I fully lost it.

He cinched down on my sides to keep me from running. "Kenna, please listen, it wasn't—"

A sob left me, cutting him off. "Don't say it. Don't you dare say it. Don't give me some stupid excuse. I . . . I don't even want to hear it. Can't hear it. Please, let me go."

"Please," Kyle begged, struggling to draw me closer. "You don't understand. Please, just listen."

I shoved his chest. "Kyle, let me go!" I screamed, verging on hysterical, this feeling that he was doing this to appease some childhood fantasy of mine making me sick.

Nausea swirled through my guts and climbed up my throat.

I was so stupid.

So stupid.

I could feel a panic attack coming on.

The kind that overwhelmed and brought me to my knees and would take days to recover from.

Shamed laughter rolled out. Who was I kidding? This was going to take a lifetime to recover from. Did anyone simply recover from their first love?

He staggered back a foot, his chest heaving, his skin lit in a golden sheen of sweat.

God, how had I ever been fool enough to think *that* was really meant for me?

I slipped off the counter, my body aching and shaking with my need for him. It only felt like another slap to the face.

I tried to sidestep him, to get away, and I was loosing another gasp when he snatched me by the wrist.

Fire raced up my arm, the man flames, my destruction, and the tears ran faster.

"Kenna, please, listen to me. I'm so sorry. Let me explain."

I jerked my arm out of his hold, chest heaving with sobs, my face a mess of snot and tears and shame. "What did you want to explain to me, Kyle? That you feel sorry for me? For the pathetic virgin who's never been kissed?"

Head shaking, I backed away. "Believe me, I don't want your pity."

If I didn't know better, I would have thought it was remorse streaking through his expression.

Unable to stand there looking at him for a second longer, I whirled around and ran for my room, slamming shut the door and locking it. I went right for the closet, barely able to see through the sheets of torment falling down my face as I pulled the suitcase from the top shelf.

I threw it onto the bed and started ripping clothes from the hangers.

I had to get out of there.

Flee.

Because I should have known better.

Should have known that dream I was having was really a nightmare.

Because girls like me?

We didn't get guys like Kyle Love.

And for the first time in my life, I wondered if I actually wanted him, anyway.

four

Kyle

God damn it.

My hands went to my hair, panic gripping me in a steel fist, heart racing from being taken from one extreme to the other.

Spirit rocketing high and then the hope of finally having her crushed into the ground.

The taste of her still danced on my tongue, every inch of my body hard to the point of painful, lust and need knotting up my stomach.

But it was the expression that had been written on her face, the misery and shame that had clouded those gorgeous features, that felt like knife wound to the gut.

I'd fucked up.

Right out of the gate.

Hurt her.

And hurting her was the last thing I wanted to do.

I sucked in a shattered breath, trying to calm the riot raging inside me, trying to give her a minute to calm down so we could have a conversation.

That was until I heard the distinct sound of hangers banging in the closet, the girl trying to subdue the sobs that were coming from her mouth.

Brutal agony.

Hell no.

I wasn't going to give up on this girl without a fight.

I flew around and rushed for her room.

Could feel the disturbance radiating from within, blasting through the closed door, so strong I didn't know how it wasn't busting from the hinges.

I pounded on the wood, friction coming from the other side, a storm descending over the two of us.

I could feel it.

Fierce and unrelenting. Something that had built for so many years, desperate to break free, demolished in one stupid mistake.

But it was my mistake.

I should have known the way this would make her feel. The way it'd make her question. Especially after everything I'd read last night, her heart and soul bared in those words, so private and sweet and heartbreaking that it'd only made me love her more.

"Go away!" she shouted, but it was a tremble of agitation, the words filled with her fears.

"No, Kenna. We need to talk."

"There isn't anything to talk about."

Refusal filled my tone. "Oh, there is plenty to talk about. You and I have been running on unfinished business since we were kids. I'm not going to pretend what just happened didn't. We're going to discuss this."

Bitter, pained laughter echoed through the separation. "What? Talk about your pity? How you want the best for me? Tell me you're happy to do me the favor? No, thank you."

Frustrated, I dropped my forehead to the door, and I could feel her frantic movements on the other side, a turbulent rampage.

"Open up," I all but growled.

No response.

I smacked my palm against the wood. "Open the fucking door, Kenna."

I was going to tell her how I felt, and I was going to do it to her face. So there would be no mistake.

Faster than I could process, the door whipped open, and I

stumbled back, caught off guard by how fucking beautiful she was. Struck by the pain rolling from her in waves. Hit by the realization that this girl needed to be carefully adored.

Not because she needed sympathy or pity.

But because she deserved to be loved in the best of ways.

"Fine, there, the door is open. Are you happy?" She was doing her best to sound firm, the girl fighting her way through her torment as she thundered by, pulling a large suitcase behind her.

I whirled around, bolting after her.

I was right at her said when I grated, "Not even close."

She squeezed her eyes for a beat, like she didn't want to look at me or acknowledge me or even hear what I had to say. She just carved an enraged path for the front door.

"You can't leave like this, Kenna. This is your home, and you're pissed, and we need to talk this out."

She flipped her head around, heartbreak roiling in those brown, sincere eyes. "I can leave, Kyle. I can leave because you don't own me. Oh, you almost did, but you don't."

Grief twisted through every line of her stunning face when she said it.

I had the staggering urge to reach out and wipe it away.

Hold all her hurt.

Be responsible for all her smiles.

Make her the fucking happiest woman who ever lived.

I just had to convince her I meant it with all of me first.

She flung the front door open and started out into the hall.

I was right on her heels as she raced down the hallway.

"You're right, I don't own you, Kenna. I don't fucking own you, but you own me." My confession was grit, scraping like razors as they raked up my throat as I scrambled to stay right behind her.

She stumbled in her haste, her shoulders riding up in surprise, but she kept going.

So did I.

I wasn't about to give up.

"You own me, Kenna. Do you fucking hear me? This wasn't some pity bullshit. And yeah, I messed up. Messed up bad. I never should have looked at your computer. There is no excuse."

She spun around, almost tripping, and shit, I had to stop myself from darting for her to keep her from falling. Wanting to protect her.

Regaining her balance, she took an aggressive step in my direction.

Hurt shook through her voice. "You looked at my personal things. Invaded my privacy. You broke my trust before I even gave it to you. I didn't give you permission to see those things. And I get it . . . I'm pathetic, right? Hopeless?"

She gestured at herself with both hands, the motion full of disgust.

I started to reject that assertion, to tell her I didn't see her as pathetic for a second, but she held up a hand.

"At least, that's the way I've felt in the past. But I don't anymore, Kyle. Yeah, there are things I struggle with that I wished I didn't have to. I wish I could go to work like everyone else and not have to fear a panic attack, and I wish I could go on a date without stumbling all over myself and making myself a fool, and I wish that you wouldn't look at me with pity."

She pressed her hands over her heart, pleading with me to get it. "Like I'm less. Like you're doing me a favor."

Grief punched a hole through my chest.

Is that the way she looked at herself? Is that the way she thought I was looking at her?

She sucked in a shattered breath. "But I know what I want, and I know what makes me happy, and I'm working on all the rest. I believe in myself. We're all a work in progress, and I've made a ton of it. And I'm not about to settle for someone who is aiming to make me feel better about myself. Bolster my confidence when I don't have any."

Her head shook, and for the first time ever, there wasn't a tentative bone in her body. The girl bleeding honestly. Not shrinking for a second.

Fuck.

I liked that, too.

"I get it." Her voice quieted. "You care about me on some level because of Vanessa. Feel obligated to me in some way. You probably really do want me to experience things I've never experienced before. But believe me when I tell you I don't want to experience those things with anyone who doesn't want me for me. I want the real deal, Kyle. I mean, for a second I thought I'd take you any way that I could have you, but that's not me, and I don't want it to be. I'm not going to cheat myself."

The softest smile tugged at the corner of my mouth, and I eased forward and inch. "You think I feel obligated to you because of my sister? Because I feel sorry for you in some way?"

Uncertainty filled her expression, and disbelieving laughter rippled up my throat, like it was trying to reach out for her, hold her, words tender in their delivery. "You do realize my sister would cut my balls off if she found out I kissed you? Skin me alive if she knew I touched you. Believe me, I'm not doing her a favor."

Kenna frowned the cutest frown.

I took another step forward, unable to stay away from this girl.

Not anymore.

Not ever again.

"She kept catching me staring at you when we were in high school. When I was nearly going crazy with how fucking bad I wanted you. Not because I felt fucking sorry for you." My face pinched in sincerity. "But because I wanted what I saw. Why do you think I called you clueless all those years?"

She wavered, her tongue darting out to wet her lips like she didn't know how to respond.

I answered for her. "Because you didn't seem to get how fucking gorgeous and appealing and perfect you were. Even if you didn't want me, I wanted you to see yourself for how amazing you were."

I dipped in closer, nose filling with the scent of this girl, my heart taking off like a gunshot. "How amazing you are. And if there is anyone around here who needs pity? It's me."

Pushing through all the boundaries, I backed her against the hallway wall. I planted my hands over her head, and she gasped a breath that I inhaled, and I ran my nose up the side of her jaw so I could murmur in her ear. "Because I've been the *pathetic* fucker who's been in love with his little sister's best friend for his entire life."

Those big brown eyes blinked a thousand times, staring up at me, her face twisting with hope and doubt. "What did you say?"

I hooked her chin with my index finger and forced her to meet the gravity in what I was about to confess. The sheer truth of it. "I'm in love with you, Kenna Myer. I'm in love with this sexy body and your gorgeous heart and your giving spirit. I've been for as long as I can remember."

I angled closer. "You want the truth? I've always been right here, waiting on the sidelines for you to see me for me, too. Not the cocky asshole who was your best friend's big brother. But as a boy who fell for a girl. Fully and wholly."

Her throat wobbled as she swallowed, emotion rising in the air and shivering in the inch that separated us, our hearts running wild, a thundering crack that ricocheted through the enclosed hall.

"Why didn't you tell me?" she whispered, those eyes a tangle of need and affection and the one thing I'd wanted for all my life.

Her love.

I wanted to sweep her up. Take her and love her right back.

But I knew we couldn't go any farther without hashing this out. Putting a nail in the questions and insecurities.

Until she was clear.

Regret tightened my chest in a vice. "Already told you, for years, Vanessa warned me off. I figured maybe you were too young for me. Too good for me. I don't fucking know. Only thing I did know was it didn't feel right to go after you. I spent a ton of years trying to forget my feelings, but it didn't change, no matter how much time went by. When I went to your and Vanessa's graduation, I decided I didn't fucking care, anymore. I was going to go for it. I came to you, remember?"

I'd been all in that night.

Put my heart on the line.

She hadn't even acknowledged it.

A frown pulled across her face, brow drawing together as she searched through her memories.

Saw the second she struck on the right one.

"After dinner," she whispered, confusion twined through her

soft voice. "Out by the pool."

I gave a tight nod. "Yeah. And you didn't say anything. I figured that was it. Killed me, but I told myself I had to finally accept that you didn't feel the same. That I had to move on because loving you hurt too much."

A single tear tracked down her cheek. "I . . . I remember I was so nervous, out there with you alone. I'm pretty sure I was basically hearing a buzz in my head and not what you were actually saying. Because what I thought you were saying couldn't have been true, you know?"

She shrugged a pained shrug. "I . . . I convinced myself I was making it up. That I was assigning a whole new meaning to what you said. That you didn't mean it like I thought."

She inhaled a shaky breath. "But then you stalked away and .. . I . . . I told myself I had to at least try. Put myself out there for the first time. It took me a couple hours, but finally I managed to gather the courage to go looking for you. I found you with Lanie." The last she choked over.

Regret blasted through my being. What the fuck had I been thinking? Acting out of pride and hurt and my pouting dick rather than with my heart and mind.

I dropped my gaze and blew out a sigh. "Shit."

Tremors rumbled through her body, old wounds that shivered and shook, never fully healed. "That broke me, Kyle. Scarred me in a way that I've yet to undo. But I know I have to. I can't let a single moment define who I am."

Her gaze dropped, the girl warring with something deep and dark, before she looked back up at me from under her lashes. So damned pretty it speared me again, an arrow through the heart. A hook in my soul.

"But that's what I just did, isn't it? I let a single moment of rejection and hurt cloud what was going on between me and you . . . and . . . and I ran because that's what I do when it gets too hard. And I don't want to be that girl, anymore. I don't want to be scared of *this*."

I reached up and brushed back a lock of hair matted to her face. "I'm so goddamn sorry that I ever caused you an ounce of pain. But I was determined that night to erase you from my heart and my psyche. To finally give up the fascination I had with you."

Sadness moved across her face, and I leaned in closer, making sure I was directly in her line of sight. "But it didn't work. Didn't work for a second. Because you were always right there, a vision of perfection. You were what I compared every other girl to, and not one of them ever had a chance of filling your shoes."

I spread my palm across her face. "I love you. I love you for real. I love you with all of me. I love you for you."

A fresh round of tears slipped down her face, and I was cupping both of her cheeks, wiping away her tears.

"I'm so in love with you, Kyle Love. I love you for you. So much it hurts. I've been aching for you my whole life, and I had no idea how to fill it."

Slammed with an onslaught of desire that could no longer be tamed, I yanked her off her feet and pinned her to the wall.

She gasped and then laughed, and she threw her arms around my shoulders. I pressed her closer to the wall and brushed my lips along the shell of her ear.

"I have a pretty good idea of how to fill it."

Shivers raced across her flesh, a palpable singe I wanted to trace with my tongue, just as badly as I wanted to devour the needy sigh that scraped her throat.

So I did.

I swallowed that sweet little sound with a kiss.

A kiss that was hard and desperate. A little manic. Two of us finally free. No walls left between us. No questions or insecurities or nosey sisters that were just going to have to get over the two of us.

Fingers dove into my hair, fisting tight, tugging hard.

Reckless and rash, pricks of pain pulling at my scalp.

The force of it shot straight to my dick.

My dick that was hard as steel. Impatient to finally get in this girl.

Her pussy hot where she was rubbing against my pants, her desire wrapping me in chains.

But I had to be careful with her.

Not because she was pathetic or fragile or weak.

But because she deserved to be treated right.

Adored and worshipped and revered.

She kissed me back with a passion unlike anything I'd ever felt.

But that's the way it was when you found your match.

It was a fire. An inferno. Fireworks launched from a deserted island. The magnitude of it hitting you from out of nowhere.

Awestruck.

Love blistered and blew, devotion pumping firm as we fought to get closer to the other.

"Kyle," she whispered. "I need you."

"I know, cupcake. You've got me. I'm yours. I'm not going anywhere."

"Actually, you are."

I jerked back to look at her.

She had a coy grin on her face. "You're taking me to my bedroom."

Shyness bled out with her demand, but that's what it was, the girl telling me what she wanted.

I was all too willing to oblige.

Still, I had to tease her a little. "Oh, yeah?"

She bit down on her bottom lip, redness splashed all over her cheeks. "Mmhmm."

I nipped that bottom lip with my teeth. "Tell me you aren't just using me for my body."

She splayed her hands over my shoulders. "I *have* spent an inordinate amount of time fantasizing about it," she rasped just under her breath.

A groan escaped.

Shit.

Wasn't sure I could handle that, the idea of this girl getting off to the memory of me.

"Then I guess it's about time you experienced the real deal."

She scratched her fingertips along the scruff of my jaw. "And I'm so, so ready."

I carried her back through the door that still sat wide open, leaving her suitcase behind.

We'd deal with that later.

We had far more important things to attend to.

I kicked shut the door as I held her by the bottom.

She giggled. God, I loved the sound of that, her joy flooding the room, as blinding as the sun that poured in through the windows. "So sexy. Just like a romance novel."

I nuzzled my entire face in her chest. "I'm about to show you a romance novel."

"Oh, I hope so."

The mood was light, the two of us finally free, no separation or worry left between us.

I carried her into her room and tossed her onto the middle of her bed. My girl bounced on the mattress, laughing and squirming and panting heavy, the girl staring up at me like she was looking at the sun.

Nerves racing fast, but trust in her eyes.

I was going to show her that she could.

I crawled over her tight little body that writhed, her hips jerking from the mattress in a bid to meet with mine.

My expression softened, adoration filling me full when I reached down and cupped the side of her face. "I love you, Kenna. Tell me you belong to me."

She touched my face. "I'm yours, Kyle Love. From here to eternity. I'm right here . . . take me."

five

Kenna

My words echoed through the space between us. I was certain they were more assured than any word I'd ever whispered or written or imagined into existence.

I lay staring up at the man who hovered over me. That presence fierce and intense and unrelenting, his gaze deep and possessive and somehow tender.

Filled with an adoration I hadn't understood before then.

Maybe it had been my insecurities. My fears. Or maybe my path had just been different. That I needed the time to grow and understand and accept who I really was and what I wanted.

And what I wanted was Kyle Love. I had always, but now, it was different.

I trembled with it.

My body a fault line getting ready to shatter.

He leaned down and kissed me.

Softly.

Lips sweet and full, an intoxicating drug that made me high, bliss filling my mind and teasing into my senses, his tongue a demand that pulsed desire through my veins.

Fear was there, too.

I realized that was okay.

It was a part of who I was. That as long a I didn't allow it to steal my joy, that it didn't take my choices, that I would accept that part of me.

Work with it.

Give pieces of it to him, knowing he would be there to help me hold them.

A big hand splayed across my face, and he tipped up my chin, taking the kiss even deeper as that muscled, lean, hard body brushed up against all my soft.

Just a tease.

My insides screamed.

A groan bled from between my lips, and I could feel him smiling against my mouth.

"Someone's anxious," Kyle murmured before he pulled back to look at me. My chest tightened as I stared up at the gorgeous man staring back at me. Dizziness swept through my mind, my equilibrium shot, everything buzzing and trembling as I teetered at the edge of the sublime.

The man had awakened every cell that had lain dormant.

Stoked a fire that had been waiting to be lit.

A hot blanket of shyness and want spread across my flesh.

Kyle watched it as if he were tracing the shape the blush painted, the man cherishing every second of me.

"I've been waiting for this for a long, long time," I whispered, making sure he knew. That he understood that he had it all. Was taking it all. That I was willingly offering it to him.

He edged off the end of the bed and straightened to his full height. His magnificent chest bare, his abs ripped and hard and packed, his *package* pressing at the thin fabric of the sleep pants that hung low on his hips.

That blush spread like a wildfire, my inexperience rustling through my nerves, all of it amplified with this need that I'd never felt before.

A glow between my thighs that made me press my heels to the bed, shifting in anticipation, deprived for too long.

"I'm pretty sure I've been waiting for this longer," he rumbled in his sexy, confident way. "Waiting for you to find me. Waiting for my match. For the person I always knew was meant for me."

His gaze swept over me where I was waiting for him on the bed.

And I didn't feel self-conscious or small. I felt like the most beautiful creature that ever existed. No longer questioning that was the way he viewed me.

"Are you nervous?" he asked, voice low and eyes keen as he watched me carefully, though there was the hint of a smile threatening at his mouth.

Just looking at him had the man pinning one to mine, the twist of my lips soft and awed and devoted.

Because oh God, was he something to look at.

And he was mine.

"Yes," I admitted, my chest heaving as I sat up a little, just wanting to be closer to him. "But I like the way it feels. The way it feels like I can't breathe while I'm waiting. I can't wait to be with you."

That smile cracked, and he reached out and touched my chin with the knuckle of his index finger.

A tender, sweet caress.

Then he edged back and started to push down the waistband of his sleep pants.

Oh my God.

I was pretty sure my mouth dropped open. I might have even drooled a little.

Could anyone blame me?

Redness streaked and bloomed, heat consuming me like I was on open flames as he bared himself to me.

Fully unclothed as he stepped out of the pants.

The man was hung like a priceless painting in a museum.

"Now I'm really starting to worry you might be using me for my body."

My attention snapped up to his face. That was a feat in itself. Then I was blushing more as I watched the smirk pull to his delicious mouth.

I rested back on my hands, flipping my hair back, going for sexy, knowing it was most likely all kinds of awkward, my heart fluttering when I realized he'd like it if it was, anyway. That he loved me for me.

"Maybe a little," I told him, letting my need rush out into the room. Desire coating the words.

He climbed onto his hands and knees on the bed, forcing me back as he came closer, crawling over the top of me.

My heart took off at a sprint, so loud I knew he could hear it, the same as I could feel his thundering from his chest.

"I guess I can be okay with that," he teased, voice a rough scrape, as rough as the hand he clenched down on my hip. "I plan on using this body for my pleasure again and again.

"Oh." It left me on a surprised gasp, then my stomach twisted in anticipation as the man's gaze went feral.

"But it's my heart that's exploding with bliss," he growled.

Savage and sweet.

Oh my.

Turned out I liked that a lot.

I wanted him rough and soft.

Demanding and giving.

He slipped his hand under my sweatshirt and spread it up my side, riding up over my ribs, until he was cupping my breast and his thumb was flicking it across my bare nipple.

Sensation flashed, and I inhaled a sharp breath, arching into his touch.

I liked that even better.

Needing more.

Needing it all.

"Look at that, Kenna. Look how your body comes alive when I touch you. Did you know it, that you were meant for me?"

"I was too scared to. Now I'm too scared to believe otherwise."

He sat back a fraction, and both his hands went to the hem of my shirt, and he slowly peeled it up, exposing me inch by inch.

Cool air struck my flesh. Goosebumps rushed, crawling across my skin like an illicit caress.

Kyle hissed as he pulled the shirt over my head, my hair getting loose and tumbling over my shoulders.

For the first time in my life, my upper body was naked in front of a man.

I wasn't scared.

I felt freed.

Liberated.

Tender fingertips trailed along my collarbone, dipping down between my breasts, and tickling across my belly. "You are stunning, Kenna. So pretty. So sexy in your shyness. So sexy in your boldness."

My teeth clamped down on my bottom lip, and emotion clawed up my throat, so thick and perfect. I reached out, tracing the defined muscles of his broad chest. "You are like a fairytale."

"A romance?" A chuckle laced his words.

I gave him a nod. "That's what it feels like. Perfect and special and bigger than life. *Impossible.*"

"Except it's not, is it?" He held himself up on his hands, crawling closer, forcing me down onto my back. He dipped down and brushed his lips over mine.

Chills tumbled and spread, need growing tenfold with every second that passed.

"This is as real as it gets, cupcake. Are you ready for it?"

Anxiety and lust and love careened through my being, crashing through every reservation. Through every fear. Through every question. Toppling them all.

Because only one answer remained.

I belonged to Kyle Love, and he belonged to me.

"Yes."

He sat back so he could peel my shorts and underwear down. I was pretty sure it took my insecurities with them.

My body alive.

Burning with a feeling unlike anything I'd felt before.

Brown eyes devoured me as if I were actually made of chocolate and frosting with a cherry on top.

He grinned a salacious grin, and my insides shivered in anticipation.

"Gorgeous girl."

Then he did devour me, without any warning, his head diving between my thighs and his tongue licking into my center.

My hips shot for the sky and I yelped with the contact.

The man blowing me right to the moon.

He held me down, keeping me from floating away, while I was sucking for the nonexistent air, all of it stolen with the immediate feeling that swept through my body.

Pinpoints of pleasure that coalesced and grew and filled me whole.

He licked at me, his tongue nothing but the definition of ecstasy, and I nearly lost my mind when he slowly pressed two fingers inside the well of my body, full and intrusive and perfect.

He drove them in and out, and that feeling rose and lifted and changed.

Grew full and intense and acute.

Until it became too much and everything was coming apart in the best way that it could.

Bliss splitting me wide open, gushing free, rushing through every nerve ending until I could feel him touching my everywhere. The man infiltrating every cell.

I was shattered.

Saved.

He was right, I came alive under his touch.

Though it felt more like an awakening.

Enlightenment.

Air raked from my lungs, chest jutting and heaving, jutting like my hips, not sure how to handle the feeling of him, the tingles and the tiny pulses of pleasure that kept rocketing through my body.

He edged up onto his knees, his hands on my belly as if he were keeping a hold on me to keep me grounded.

Sure I was going to float away.

But I wasn't going anywhere.

"I need to get a condom," he murmured, glancing over his shoulder in the vague direction of his bag I knew was still sitting on the floor in the other room, and I was flapping an arm at my nightstand. "I have some."

He quirked brow, but it was cute and adoring. "Prepared for me?"

"I told you I liked living in a fantasy."

"That's my girl."

That's my girl.

Those butterflies flapped contented wings.

Kyle leaned up so he could rummage through the drawer, all too quick to produce a condom that he was tearing from the foil and rolling over his massive, hard penis that bobbed and jerked against his ripped stomach.

Redness climbed my cheeks. It was true. This man was the best kind of a fantasy.

The kind that became reality.

Another rush of need tumbled through my body, that achy spot between my thighs throbbing with anticipation, and I rubbed my knees together to try to sate the hunger.

I guessed he made me greedy.

Kyle set his hands on my shaky knees, and he spread them, a grin on his ridiculously handsome face as he seated himself there, though his expression turned tender as he lowered himself against me, his golden skin brushing mine, filling me with fire and hope and awe.

"Thank you choosing me, Kenna. For letting it be me. For finding me."

"I think it was you who came to find me."

Threading the fingers of one hand through my hair, he dipped down close, his words rustling across my face like a promise. "Where else would I have gone? I think you were always calling out for me."

He nestled deeper between my thighs, our abdomen's touching, the hardness of him pressing at my achy, desperate center.

"Imagined this a million times, Kenna. Kissing you. Loving you. Touching you." He dipped down and brushed his mouth along the shell of my ear. "Fucking you."

Shivers rolled, a crashing wave of seduction and desire and torment.

My fingers sank into his shoulders, gripping onto him, and he gathered me in an arm, hugging me close to the roaring pulse that sped through his veins.

Then he took me.

Quickly.

Stealing my breath, filling me with his as he stilled, my body overcome by his.

He gripped me and held me and whispered my name again and again.

"I have you," he murmured. "I have you. Are you okay?"

My forehead nodded against his, the two of us frozen in that moment of time, staring at the other, silent promises whispered into eternity.

"More than okay," I finally told him as the shock and pain wore off, as something trickled in to replace it. "Perfect."

Never had I felt so exposed.

So real.

So adored.

So loved by this man.

The only one with the power to peel back my layers and expose what was underneath. The only one strong enough to fight me on my fears.

To chase me right up to the edge and then tumble over the side with me.

A freefall where we got lost.

"I love you, Kenna," he murmured, then he kissed me slow, made love to me sweetly.

Carefully.

Tenderly.

Our bodies in sync. This rhythm that struck in the atmosphere.

It was complete, utter magic.

He kissed along my jaw, and I felt the muscles on his back tighten, his movements coming harder and more rigid. "I want to stay in you forever, but you feel too good," he groaned before he pulled back to cast me a gentle smile.

Adoration ridged his lips and flamed in his eyes.

I ran my fingers along the defined line of his striking jaw. "I'm yours forever."

With my words, Kyle let go, his thrusts coming fast and hard and demanding, the man gazing down at me as his hips drove and rocked. Until his face twisted and a moan that was my name was coming from his mouth and his body was going ridged.

He pulsed and jerked and twitched, a slew of silent curses coming off his tongue that were nothing but praise, and I was certain there was no better sight than watching this man come apart.

He slumped down on me, pressed is nose into my hair, his breaths choppy and rough as he struggled to come down. I could feel him grinning at the side of my face. "That's right you are. I'm gonna keep you, Kenna Cupcake."

It was a sweet, sweet tease.

Love blossomed all over my body. So huge I was sure it had become its own entity.

"I like the sound of that."

The front door banged open. My eyes went wide with fear, and Kyle was whirling around, putting is whole body in between me and whoever had come inside.

"Hello? Kenna? Why the hell is there a suitcase out in the hall and the door's unlocked?"

Vanessa.

She wasn't supposed to be back for two days.

Was it bad I wished we were getting broken into instead? Because this was . . . mortifying.

"What are we supposed to tell her?" I mouthed in horror.

Kyle grinned. "We tell her what I should have told her a long time ago."

He hopped off the bed, shucked the condom, tossed it into the garbage, and tugged on his pants. He was already staggering out my bedroom door before I could stop him.

"Kyle . . . what the hell?" Vanessa screeched, her voice coming clearer now that my door was wide open.

"Hello, little sister."

"What's going on?" I couldn't see her, but I was pretty sure she was planting her hands on her hips, suspicion filling her tone.

Kyle peeked back at me from where he was in the hall, sending me a slow smile before he was turning back to her. "What do you think of officially welcoming Kenna into the family. She's pretty much been her whole life, anyway. Sound like a good plan, Kenna Cupcake?" he asked, swinging his attention back to me, smirking with all that easy confidence that he wore like a brand.

Then his smirk softened into something real, exposing the sincerity in the question.

Oh my God.

Kyle Love was gonna marry me.

It was true what they said. There was just something about a hot a guy. Something that made you itchy and anxious. Smitten.

Only this one was mine.

And I wasn't ever going to let him go.

the end

Thank you for reading *Something About a Hot Guy*!
I hope you loved this fun novella!.

More from A.L. Jackson

<u>*Hollywood Chronicles, a collaboration with USA Today Bestselling Author, Rebecca Shea*</u>
One Wild Night
One Wild Ride

ABOUT THE AUTHOR

A.L. Jackson is the New York Times & USA Today Bestselling author of contemporary romance. She writes emotional, sexy, heart-filled stories about boys who usually like to be a little bit bad.

Her bestselling series include THE REGRET SERIES, CLOSER TO YOU, BLEEDING STARS, FIGHT FOR ME, and CONFESSIONS OF THE HEART.

If she's not writing, you can find her hanging out by the pool with her family, sipping cocktails with her friends, or of course with her nose buried in a book.

Be sure not to miss new releases and sales from A.L. Jackson - Sign up to receive her newsletter http://smarturl.it/NewsFromALJackson or text "aljackson" to 33222 to receive short but sweet updates on all the important news.

Connect with A.L. Jackson online:

Page **http://smarturl.it/ALJacksonPage**
Newsletter **http://smarturl.it/NewsFromALJackson**
Angels **http://smarturl.it/AmysAngelsRock**
Amazon **http://smarturl.it/ALJacksonAmzn**
Book Bub **http://smarturl.it/ALJacksonBookbub**
Text "aljackson" to 33222 to receive short but sweet updates on all the important news.

www.ingramcontent.com/pod-product-compliance
Lightning Source LLC
Chambersburg PA
CBHW032043180726
48284CB00008B/2730